Henry and Sara

Written by: Lisa Kelly

Illustrations by Destiny Nagle

Henry and Sara

Written by:	Lisa Kelly and
Co-authored By:	Barbara Jean Nagle
Illustrated by:	Destiny Jean Nagle and Barbara Jean Nagle
Edited By:	Jenna Marie Tedesco

First Printing 2015

HENRY AND SARAH

Published In Loving Memory Of Lisa Kelly
Dedicated To Her Daughter, Zoe

Written by Lisa Jean Kelly at age 27 in 2002

INTRODUCTION

Introduction by: Jenna Marie Tedesco & Barbara Jean Nagle
(with a little help from the breezes :-))

Henry and Sara tells a heartwarming story of love, loss and everlasting friendship.

In this refreshingly simple storybook, we are taken on a playful journey with two dear rabbit friends. A story that has played a very real part in the lives of those who knew and deeply love the author, Lisa Jean Kelly.

Henry and Sara is a gentle, enchanting journey that explores the delicacy of life and death. Readers are comforted with playful symbolism while being introduced to transcendental concepts of eternity, spirituality, friendship and the immortality of love.

The breezes mentioned are living memories that Lisa left behind. They are tiny vases filled with red carnations, tea parties, Dave & Busters, Disney World, Johnny Rockets and all the other places throughout the world that Lisa explored.

The breezes are in the memories of Ozzfest and Cirque du Soleil. They grow within the irises and purple asters that adorn the Japanese garden Lisa planted next to her home.

Lisa's loving breezes are alive in the hearts of her yoga students and Reiki patients. They continue to whisper around those that she healed with her hands, her heart and with her gracious, compassionate spirit. They flow through the many poems Lisa wrote in her journals, they are sweet memories for Zoe and all of us that she continues to touch so dearly even after death.

Lisa, like Sara continues to protect, enlighten and guide those she kept near and dear, we can hear her and feel her close.

As you are reading her story, perhaps you may even feel her gentle breeze as she lovingly graces you in appreciation.

Henry and Sara lived in the same meadow.

They were the best of friends.

Henry and Sara spent all their days playing together.
They shared secrets and lots of laughs.

Once while under the big oak tree, they made a promise that they
would always be together.

Henry was younger than Sara, and did not remember
ever playing without her.

They truly were the best of friends.

One day, something strange happened.

Sara was not under the big oak tree
waiting to play with Henry.

After waiting for ten minutes, which seemed like hours to him,
Henry went to Sara's den to find her.

When Henry found Sara, she was still in bed.
Henry tried to get her up, but she was too tired.

She did not want to run and play. She only wanted to rest.

Henry could not understand why Sara did not want to play.

Henry could not imagine playing without her, so he lay down
beside her, and there he waited.

The next morning, Henry was still waiting for Sara to get out of bed. Sara finally opened her eyes and spoke softly saying:

"Henry, my friend, I am older than you, and the time is near for me to join the other rabbits in the Great Meadow."

Henry did not understand. He looked puzzled and scared.

"You are leaving our meadow? Where is the Great Meadow? Can I come with you? What about our promise?"

Sara interrupted Henry's questions,

"I made a promise that I intend to keep.
My friendship and love are forever.
I will always be near you, like a cool breeze upon your ears."

Those were the last words Sara spoke.

Henry held Sara's limp body.

He cried and cried throughout the whole day.

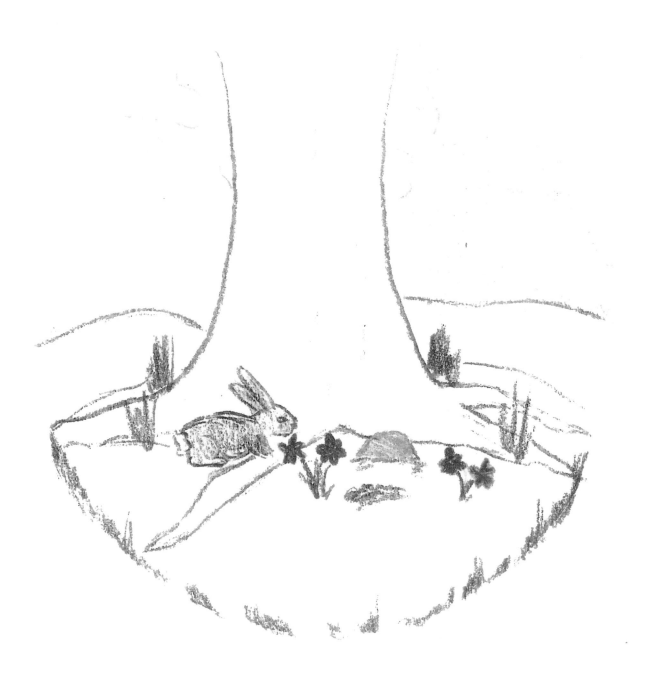

The next day when no more tears would come, he took Sara's
body to the big oak tree and prepared a special resting place.
Then he found a beautiful shiny stone by the brook and placed
it under the tree for her.

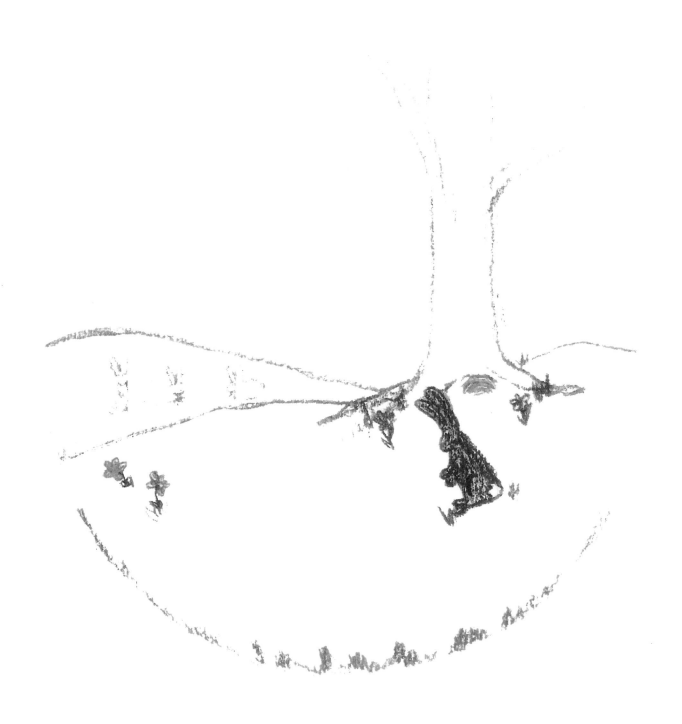

Every day Henry sat under the big oak tree.

He did not run and play with the other rabbits.

He was sooooo sad for he missed his best friend very much.

One day, while on his way to the big oak tree,
Henry felt a strange breeze across his face and whiskers.

Then it circled around his ears.
It felt like a big soft hug.

Henry looked up into the sky.

His heart beat rapidly, and tears of joy ran down his face.

Henry now knew that Sara had kept her promise

And would always be with him.

And she was.

Made in the USA
Charleston, SC
17 November 2015